HIPPOS GO BERSERK

Written and Illustrated by

Sandra Boynton

Little, Brown and Company

Boston   Toronto

To Rags
(from Riches)

Library of Congress Cataloging in Publication Data

Boynton, Sandra.
   Hippos go berserk.

   SUMMARY: Larger and larger groups of hippos join
a lone hippopotamus for a night-time party.
   [1. Hippopotamus-Fiction.   2. Counting.   3. Stories
in rhyme]   I. Title.
PZ8.3.B7Hi   [E]   79-16134
ISBN 0-316-10488-4
ISBN 0-316-10489-2 pbk.

Published simultaneously in Canada
by Little, Brown & Company (Canada) Limited

PRINTED IN THE UNITED STATES OF AMERICA

One hippo, all alone,

calls two hippos

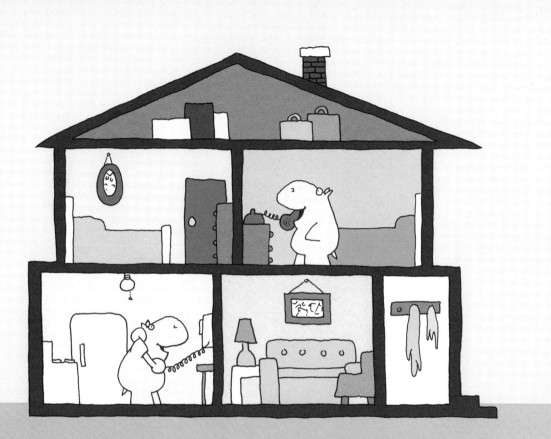

on the phone.

Three hippos at the door

bring along another four.

Five hippos come overdressed.

Six hippos show up with a guest.

Seven hippos

arrive in a sack.

Eight hippos
sneak in the back.

Nine hippos

come to work.

ALL THE HIPPOS

GO BERSERK !

All through the hippo night,
  hippos play with great delight.

But at the hippo break of day,
  the hippos all must go away.

Nine hippos and a beast join

eight hippos riding east, while

seven hippos moving west leave

six hippos quite distressed, and

five hippos then set forth with

four hippos headed north.

Three hippos say, "Good day."

The last two hippos go their way.

One hippo, alone once more,

misses the other forty-four.